Hey Freddy, it's Canada's Birthday!

Story by
Susan Chalker Browne

Illustrations by
HildaRose

Freddy woke up in the dark.
Down the hall, he could hear
Baby Clare crying.

He jumped out of bed, brushed his teeth, then raced back to his room and dressed in his Mountie outfit.

He pulled on black pants with a bright yellow stripe down the side. Zipped up a red hoodie and fastened a wide belt round his waist. Yanked on rubber boots right up to his knees and fixed a brown Stetson on his head. Two white gloves on his hands and he was all set to go.

"Freddy?" His mom poked her head into the room. "Are you ready?"

"All ready!" said Freddy, cheerfully.

The brown hat worn by Mounties is called a 'Stetson'.

The Metrobus chugged and puffed its way up Signal Hill.
People chattered and laughed and drank Tim Horton's
coffee.

Freddy sipped on his juice box, watching through the
window. Like a magic wand, the pink dawn touched the
trees and rocks with a rosy glow. "Hmm," he thought.
"I guess that's why they call it a Sunrise Ceremony."

Meanwhile Clare squalled and screeched,
while Freddy's parents fluttered and fussed.

The lower part of Signal Hill Road
was once called Vinnicomb's Hill.

The Signal Hill parking lot was packed with people. Freddy leaped from the bus. Behind him, his mom and dad lugged blankets, bottles, backpacks and Baby Clare.

"Whoa!" exclaimed Freddy, looking all around.

An enormous brass band was setting up beside the powder house, everyone wearing striped fleece hats with floppy white tassels. Nearby stood a teenage choir, laughing and drinking hot chocolate. Clowns skipped and bounced, handing out candy and Canadian flags.

"Hey, thanks!" smiled Freddy, as a blue-haired clown popped a small flag into his hand.

The Imperial Powder Magazine, also known as the powder house, is so named because it was once used to store gunpowder.

"Freddy, is that you? Gee, I like your costume, wish I had one like that." It was William from school.

"William! Hi! Isn't this cool?"

"Sure is," said William. "Wow. What's wrong with her?" He pointed at Clare.

"Oh, that's just Clare. She's cranky."

"Hmm," replied William. "Maybe this will cheer her up." He waved a Canadian flag. Two silver bells attached to the top tinkled and plinked.

Instantly Clare stopped crying and her tiny hands reached out for William's flag. Freddy's mom and dad stared at the flag hopefully.

The current Canadian flag was first flown on February 15, 1965, a day celebrated each year as Flag Day.

"William," said Freddy's dad, slowly. "Would you mind if we borrowed that flag?"

"I guess," said William, reluctantly, as he handed it to Clare.

But just then, a gust of wind curled off the ocean and whipped the flag high in the air.

"Whoa!" cried Freddy, as the flag somersaulted over their heads. "Hey, William—let's get it!" And the two boys broke into a run.

Behind them, Clare bellowed and bawled, her face as purple as a plum.

"That's my special flag," shouted William. "My granny got it for me in Ottawa!"

Signal Hill is located at the edge of the Atlantic Ocean.

Bouncing, tumbling, twisting and turning, the flag tinkled and plinked on the clear morning air. Suddenly it dove from the sky. And stuck in a lady's grey bun.

"Excuse me, Ma'am," said Freddy, as he and William skidded to a stop. "Do you know there's a flag in your hair?"

"My goodness, so there is!" said the lady with the grey bun, as she patted her head. But just as she was about to pluck it out, a gust of wind curled off the ocean and whipped the flag high in the air.

"Hey William—let's get it!" yelled Freddy.

In Newfoundland, July 1st is also called Memorial Day, a day we remember WWI soldiers killed at Beaumont Hamel in 1916.

Bouncing, tumbling, twisting and turning, the flag tinkled and plinked on the clear morning air. Suddenly it dove from the sky. And stuck in a tall man's trumpet.

"Excuse me, Sir," said Freddy, as he and William skidded to a stop. "Do you know there's flag in your trumpet?"

"My goodness, so there is!" exclaimed the trumpet player. But just as he was about to pluck it out, a gust of wind curled off the ocean and whipped the flag high in the air.

"Hey William—let's get it!" yelled Freddy.

The first transatlantic wireless signal was received on top of Signal Hill by Guglielmo Marconi, on December 12, 1901.

Bouncing, tumbling, twisting and turning, the flag tinkled and plinked on the clear morning air. Suddenly it dove from the sky. And stuck in a tourist's backpack.

"Excuse me, Miss," said Freddy, as he and William skidded to a stop. "Do you know there's a flag in your backpack?"

"My goodness, so there is!" cried the tourist, turning round to see. But just as she was about to pluck it out, a gust of wind curled off the ocean and whipped the flag high in the air.

"Hey William—let's get it!" yelled Freddy.

Signal Hill received its name from the practice of flag signalling to announce the arrival of ships.

Bouncing, tumbling, twisting and turning, the flag tinkled and plinked on the clear morning air. Suddenly it dove from the sky. And stuck in a patch of grass.

"Finally!" said Freddy, as he and William skidded to a stop. But just as Freddy was about to pluck it out, a saucy black crow swept from the sky, snatching William's flag.

"Oh no!" shouted Freddy and William.

The crow whooshed high over Signal Hill, circled, soared and swooped, then sailed to the very tip-top of Cabot Tower, the flag trapped in its beak.

Cabot Tower was built between 1897 and 1900, to honour both Queen Victoria and explorer John Cabot.

The band started up—all the trombones and trumpets and big snare drums bursting into music. Joyfully, the choir sang 'O Canada' and the entire crowd joined in. Even the saucy crow wanted to sing. "Caw!" it squawked, as it flapped its wings and lifted off, dropping the flag to the ground.

William grabbed it and raced to Clare, pressing it into her open hands. Instantly Clare stopped crying. Freddy's mom and dad were very relieved.

Suddenly there was another sound. At first, Freddy wasn't sure what it was.

'O Canada' was proclaimed Canada's national anthem on July 1st, 1980, one hundred years after it was first sung.

"Is that a horse?" he asked William. "I think I hear a horse!"

At that very moment, an enormous black horse stepped up from the road, a real live Mountie on its back. Then a second horse appeared, and a third. Soon a very long, very straight line of horses and Mounties were parading around Signal Hill.

"It's the Musical Ride!" cried a man wearing a yellow toque.

Freddy's mouth hung open and he stared. Never before had he seen so many Mounties. They marched their horses neatly round the parking lot, right toward him.

The horses of the Musical Ride are black, as a pleasing contrast to the RCMP red tunics.

"Well, what have we here?" asked the lead rider, pulling his horse to a stop. "A Mountie with no horse? How would you like to share mine?" And he bent over, scooped Freddy up and sat him in the saddle.

"Whoa!" exclaimed Freddy, looking all around.

The Royal Canadian Mounted Police was formed in 1873 to preserve peace on the Canadian frontier.

The horses swished their tails, shuffled and pawed the ground. Prancing in time to the music they moved into a design of four circles, trotting round and round. Then they created the swinging gates. After that, a moving wagon wheel. And all this time Freddy was first in line, strutting along on the biggest horse of all.

"Happy Canada Day!" he shouted, grinning and waving at Mom, Dad, Clare and William too. The trombones boomed, the choir sang, the crowd cheered, and sunlight danced on the sparkling ocean.

On October 27, 1982, July 1st
—then known as Dominion Day—
was renamed Canada Day.

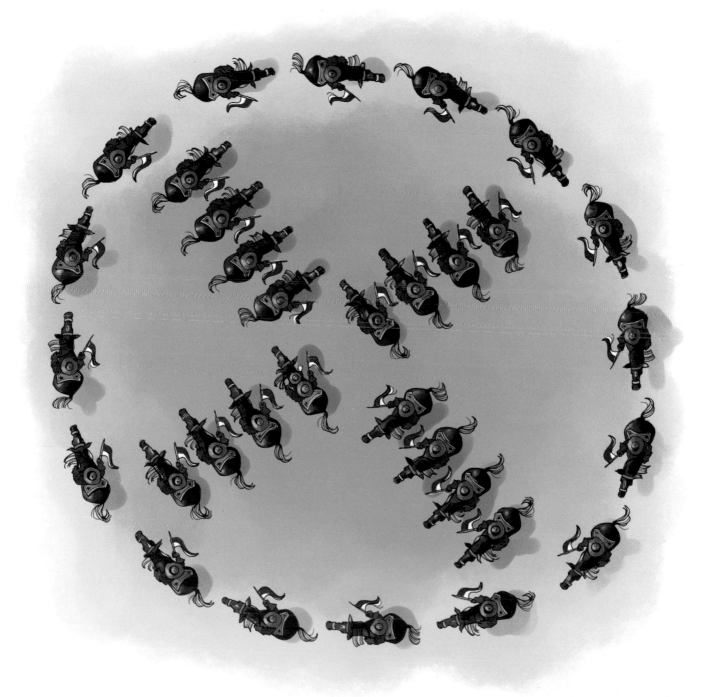

Canada Council **Conseil des Arts**
for the Arts **du Canada**

Newfoundland
Labrador

We gratefully acknowledge the financial support of
The Canada Council for the Arts, the Government
of Canada through the Book Publishing Industry
Development Program (BPIDP), and the Government of
Newfoundland and Labrador through the Department
of Tourism, Culture and Recreation for our publishing
program.

Illustrations ©2009, Kathy (HildaRose) Kaulbach
Design and layout by Kathy Kaulbach

Published by

Tuckamore Books
a Creative Publishers imprint

A Transcontinental Inc. associated company
P.O. Box 8660, Station A
St. John's, Newfoundland A1B 3T7

Printed in Canada by: Transcontinental Inc.

Library and Archives Canada Cataloguing in Publication

Browne, Susan Chalker, 1958-
Hey Freddy, it's Canada's Birthday!
/ story by Susan Chalker Browne ; illustrations by HildaRose.

ISBN 978-1-897174-39-5

1. Canada Day--Juvenile fiction. I. Rose, Hilda, 1955-
II. Title.

PS8553.R691H49 2009   jC813'.6   C2009-902327-X